My career as a professional golfer has allowed me to experience many privileged events. I have traveled to many places around the world and competed on the finest courses. These courses are usually maintained to the highest standards with barely a blade of grass out of place.

While competing in tournaments, success depends on a good game plan and great execution. When improper execution causes a professional golfer to spend a little extra mental energy escaping trouble, he must do so with the least amount of penalty. You could say he wants to get back to his own little world quickly.

While reading about Ajene Jabari, I noticed he was probably playing a golf course much like the ones I have played in my travels. I have not experienced what Ajene was faced with when he hit his ball out of play that day. His mind nor his heart could escape what he encountered when he met a very poor boy named Moses. Ajene later finished his round, but he knew he would never be the same.

Take a journey and discover what happens to Ajene in the pages that follow. It is my hope that you will be inspired to reach out to those in need. I believe there is no greater calling in life.

—Lee Janzen
Two-Time U.S. Open Champion

I spend much of my life now traveling the world as a UNICEF Goodwill Ambassador. One of the most impressive things I've ever seen is Feed The Children's work among children who have been orphaned by AIDS in Africa. I'm not telling you what I've heard. I'm telling you what I've seen.

—Sir Roger Moore

Athletic competition has been my life. You're holding a book about innocent children who are losing the competition to stay alive. This is not about anybody's game.

—Shaquille O'Neal

Sometimes God writes a better script than anyone else can write it. The truth is sometimes stranger and more poignant than fiction, and this is one of those stories.

—Louis Gossett Jr.

This story will grip your heart and never let go. You will discover that love lives even in the darkness of a world filled with hateful neglect. Larry Jones shows us all how to find life, just when we think it is too late.

—Jack Graham
Pastor, Prestonwood Baptist Church

I Lost My Ball And Found My Life

I Lost My Ball And Found My Life

LARRY JONES

CREATION
HOUSE

A STRANG COMPANY

I Lost My Ball and Found My Life by Larry Jones
Published by Creation House
A Strang Company
600 Rinehart Road
Lake Mary, Florida 32746
www.creationhouse.com

Unless otherwise noted, all Scripture quotations are from the Holy Bible, New International Version of the Bible. Copyright © 1973, 1978, 1984, International Bible Society. Used by permission.

Cover images by Sean Kelley
Design Director: Bill Johnson
Cover designer: Amanda Potter

Library of Congress Control Number: 2008939237
International Standard Book Number:
978-1-59979-534-8

First Edition

08 09 10 11 12 — 987654321
Printed in the United States of America

Dedicated to AIDS orphans who
struggle to stay alive

PREFACE

A FEW MILES BEYOND DOWNTOWN NAIROBI'S clamor of traffic and toxic fumes, tangled clusters of brush dot the face of a steeply rising slope. The otherwise barren incline culminates in a plateau conspicuously devoid of any sign of life—plant or animal. At first glance, the rise presents itself as a serene escape from the city's helter-skelter absorption of Western culture. From the crest, however, you'll see a Kenyan game preserve about a mile away as the crow flies where elephants, lions, and assorted beasts of prey lurk. When the wind is right, you can hear the king of the jungle roar within his domain.

Should you turn about face from there, you'll behold the dark secret hidden by the mountain. A red brick building stands nondescript in its relentless symmetry up to the edge of a flat roof. You might assume it's a schoolhouse until you notice the vertical bars across its broken windows and realize it's a prison. Listen closely and you'll likely hear human screams. You will recognize the hysterical pleading of the women, dragged into the confinement barely alive and likely to be carried out dead. Come nightfall, the wailing wafts across the mountain, hanging heavy in the air with the acrid stench of cruelty and injustice.

With another turn, you'll see the rotting and violent slum called Kibera extending from right to left at the bottom of the rise as far as the eye can see. You may never have seen anything so vast. Come sundown, when Kibera's legion of sexual predators prowl, the tortured laments of Kiberan women rise in concert with those of the female inmates up on the mountain. Bars imprison the latter, poverty the former; but the effect is much the same.

Adjacent to it all, still another setting is visible from the plateau's lofty perch—a lush paradise of manicured greens and civilized finery where the masters of Kenya's upper class play golf. It is there that you will meet Ajene Jabari, one of those masters. Within these pages, he'll unwittingly slice his ball across a wall that separates his world of privilege from that of Kibera's hopelessness and depravity. You'll accompany him as he crosses that barrier to retrieve his ball—and thus crosses into a landscape of misery and terror that civilized people can scarcely imagine. He'll find himself shocked and morally challenged. But, in the end, he'll discover compassion within himself that he never knew he possessed.

Maybe you will, too.

CHAPTER ONE

Rich and poor have this in common: The
*L*ORD *is the Maker of them all.*
— PROVERBS 22:2

AJENE HAD SWUNG HIS FIVE-IRON TOO FORCE-fully, attempting to chip onto a green he'd overshot. Thus, he overshot again. His ball bounced down the sloping knoll then hopped over the block wall that had been erected years ago as a barrier between his privileged world and Kibera.

"I'll be lucky to triple-bogey on this hole," he fussed to himself.

The wall had no gate. People on the "safe" side would never have tolerated one, as a gate might have tempted desperate and starving Kiberans to venture into the pristine world of the rich.

Ajene's thoughts didn't dwell on the wall. They were set single-mindedly on the recovery of his golf ball. Sure—he had lots of other balls in his golf bag. But he had never lost a ball. And he wasn't about to start today. His mind was set on retrieving the ball from Kibera's side of the wall so he could resume play on his side. But how was he going to do it? His ball was somewhere in a slum that he had always refused to look at, much less enter. The people there were all famished and violent, he'd read. But that was *their* problem. Surely one of them had his ball. And that was creating a problem for *him.*

"Isn't that just like poor people," said one of his buddies. "They are starving to death, and so they steal a golf ball. They'd rather steal than eat."

Ajene peered over the wall into the squalor and, for the first time, focused on the mud dwellings, the barren land, and the slow walk of Kibera's emaciated inhabitants.

"They even look like they're starving," Ajene remarked.

"That's not our problem," said another golfer.

But for an instant, Ajene wondered just whose problem it was.

* * * *

Ajene heard him before he saw him—a child whose feet pounded the hardened ground as he dashed toward the wall on its Kiberan side. As he approached, the barrier hid him from view. Curious to see what the youngster was up to, Ajene backed up the slope on the golf course for a more elevated view. From there, an encompassing panorama of the desperate slum lay before him.

Still, he could only hear the child. He couldn't see what he was doing at the base of the wall on the Kibera side.

As Ajene's eyes scanned the sad vista, he recognized what he surmised to be a school yard and a tumbledown structure that might have been classrooms.

"Is anybody over there?" Ajene surprised himself

when he yelled for the boy. "Hey, I heard you. Are you there?"

"I can't see you," he continued. "You're too short. Go get a chair and stand on it."

In seconds, the lad darted into Ajene's line of sight, dashed across the yard and returned with a chair. He placed it opposite the point where Ajene stood and rose to peer over what, to him, was a towering barrier.

His small, dirty face cautiously met Ajene's quizzical stare.

"Did you see one of these?" the golfer asked. He held up a golf ball, and cautiously approached the wall. "It's my ball and it's lost," the golfer added.

Wordless, the child dipped out of sight. Ajene heard swishing of tall grass and assumed the boy must be searching. This small stand of wild growth was the only thing left with enough density to conceal the ball. All other plant life on Kibera's landscape had been scavenged by starving people.

With no response from the boy forthcoming, Ajene began to search on his side of the wall, although he didn't know why. He remained certain

16

that he'd seen the ball drop into the slum. For an instant, he thought about just moving on to the next hole—breaking his tradition of never having lost a ball. But that would mean he'd have to stop bragging about it—unless he lied. But that wouldn't be the same. Any golfer could lie. In fact, most of them did. And Ajene prided himself on being a cut above the rest.

Suddenly, he wanted this lost ball more than ever. It might be there in weeds. Or it might be in the hand of some Kiberan who didn't even know what he held.

One thing was certain: the ball wasn't with its owner. And nobody had the right to steal, Ajene said to himself, especially people whose station in life was far below his.

"You have a superiority complex," his conscience silently whispered.

"I sure do," the golfer responded aloud, talking to no one. "I'm better than these sick and pathetic people, and anybody would know it."

Ajene could hear the boy traipsing through the

narrow plot of grass on the other side. But no matter where he stood, he still couldn't see him.

Just then, like a human jack-in-the-box, the child's face reappeared above the palisade. In his hand, he waved a golf ball.

Ajene simultaneously felt an uncomfortable mixture of pleasure and guilt. He'd been on the brink of accusing the lad of thievery. And here the boy, who had nothing, had gone out of his way to help Ajene—a wealthy stranger—achieve his goal of finding and retrieving the ball.

Meanwhile the boy stood transfixed, staring with fascination at the white and shining sphere in his hand. Clearly he'd never seen anything like it.

Ajene called again to the boy, but it was as if the lad couldn't hear. He seemed spellbound by the uniformly indented perfection of the ball. Repeatedly he stroked the hard surface with a touch that seemed oddly affectionate—as if the ball were alive, like a pet.

The youngster clearly didn't know what to do with his find.

Leaping down from his perch, he hurled the ball

straight down onto the rigid ground—from which it instantly bounced into his face.

"That had to hurt!" Ajene said to himself, waiting for the lad's tears that never came.

The boy's startled expression morphed instead into a face-splitting grin.

"The ball bit me," he mumbled in astonishment. Ajene had read how Kiberan youngsters often play with discarded, deflated soccer balls. Apparently this child had never seen a ball that actually bounced.

The boy made a game of bouncing and chasing the golf ball.

He planted his feet, raised his arm and again thrust it downward.

In a split second, he jumped aside, making room for the bounce to shoot skyward. His play brought his uproarious laughter—which seemed to surprise him. Laughter, especially his own, was an unfamiliar sound.

Ajene's annoyance increased with the youngster's glee. This dirty, worthless child was holding up his golf game. He wanted his ball back and told the other players that he was ready to scale the wall to get it.

"Do that and those shiftless people will come from everywhere," one said. "You might as well hand them your watch and wallet."

Then his golf mates began to taunt him.

"What's the matter, Ajene?" one of them teased. "Cat got your tongue, or has a little boy got your ball?"

Ajene's temper started to boil at this intentional sneer. He didn't like to be teased and hated to be ridiculed.

"We've got to get going," one of the golfers complained.

"The guys behind us want to play through."

The words pushed Ajene's wrath into fury. There was acid in his voice as he beckoned the boy to the wall. The child glanced at the golfer timidly, and then seemed to stiffen. He was fearful, and it showed.

"You're too harsh," one of the golfers said. "These kids don't ever talk to men. Their dads run off, and they talk to women and other kids. You're scaring the little urchin."

Ajene realized his buddy was right. He was probably the first man outside Kibera who'd ever spoken to the boy. The child felt intimidated. He didn't know how to move beyond fear into conversation.

The frustrated golfer wondered if the lad had ever been beyond Kibera's borders. He flashed on articles he'd read about Kibera's demographics. Half of the residents were under sixteen years of age. The majority of the others were young and middle-aged women. Men were a conspicuous minority.

None of this was anything Ajene wanted to broach with a child who was afraid of him. The boy just stared blankly when asked his age. The more he was encouraged not to be scared, the more fearful he seemed to become.

"My name is Moses," the lad finally uttered, his gaze downcast.

The youngster studied Ajene's hands, then his own. Clearly he was comparing the golfer's neat, trim cleanliness with his own shabby filth. Ajene looked Moses up and down. He wore a tattered school uniform. The golfer had heard that the uniform was the only clothing most Kiberan children had to their name. *Was this true of Moses?* he wondered. But not for long. Pondering such things was a waste of precious time. Ajene was unaccustomed to others foiling his plans—especially those with no means and less importance.

"Give me my ball!" Ajene shouted abruptly. The boy merely winced, making no gesture to surrender it.

Ajene pulled the wallet from his hip pocket and unfolded a bill worth one hundred shillings—about $1.35 in American currency. He told the boy he could have it in exchange for the ball.

Moses's astonished expression indicated he'd never previously seen that much money. But then he'd also never beheld the seemingly magical qualities of the golf ball—a ball that bounced so high and wouldn't deflate.

"I'd rather keep the ball," Moses told the rich man.

Perturbed, Ajene held up another paper shilling. Moses again said that he'd rather retain the ball.

"Good fortune let me find it on the ground," the child said.

Ajene surmised Moses hadn't made the connection between himself—Ajene, the golfer—and the ball. From his vantage point in Kibera, perhaps Moses had seen golfers from afar, swinging glistening sticks but never knowing why. From that distance, he'd probably never seen the tiny and speeding balls, the objects of the golfers' quest.

The boy had simply scurried to a mysterious object that had penetrated his world. Then he'd seen a man approach who came from outside that world. The child didn't deduce that the ball belonged to the man. Moses assumed the stranger carrying a bag with shiny steel poles had seen the wondrous ball and simply wanted it too. And now he was offering to trade paper in exchange.

Ajene sighed and wondered—maybe this kid has a conscience? If so, he'd play on it, and coerce the return of his ball. So what if it meant the loss of

Moses's only joy? He was a Kiberan. It wasn't as if the starkly poor had any right to expect fairness from the privileged.

"When this kid grows up," Ajene pondered, "he'll come to understand that he's poor and the poor are beneath the rich. They should never expect fairness. That just isn't real."

Ajene felt peeved at himself for thinking too much. He needed to find a way to trick the worthless urchin into surrendering the golf ball and be on his way. To him, the kid was just another Kiberan contributing to the population explosion.

* * * *

Ready to try anything, Ajene began lying to Moses. He told him he had a little boy at home just like him. He even told Moses he thought he'd like his little boy, and asked if he'd like to go home with him.

"You'll like my house," Ajene continued. "It has fresh water that you can drink and it won't make

24

you sick. Inside, it's cool, even more than yours after rain. It has food—all you can eat."

"Is this house in America?" Moses asked.

"No," Ajene replied. "It's right here in Nairobi."

"But not in Kibera?" Moses probed further. His pronunciation of *Kibera* sounded more English than Swahili. Ajene attributed this to the influence of American humanitarian workers who often visited the slum.

"No," Ajene said, "my house isn't in Kibera. And the ball you're holding belongs to my son. He'll be sad when I tell him you wouldn't give it back. It's the only ball he has."

Ajene recalled that in Kibera, stealing is punishable by vigilante law. He'd read about men who were burned alive for stealing food for their families. He surmised that children, from an early age, must be taught not to steal anything, no matter how insignificant.

"You're stealing what doesn't belong to you if you keep my little boy's ball," Ajene pressed.

His guilt trip appeared to be working.

Moses began choking back tears, and finally let them flow. He was sobbing by the time he finished the short walk back to the wall. He didn't want to return the shiny ball, as he was sure it was harder and faster than any other in Kibera. He'd never seen one like it. He was certain he never would again.

But he didn't want to steal. His mother, who was very sick, had told him about God and how His feelings become sad when little boys steal.

> He who has been stealing must steal no longer, but must work, doing something useful with his own hands, that he may have something to share with those in need.
> —Ephesians 4:28

Her constant teaching about honesty had set deep roots in Moses's young conscience.

"I'm sorry," Moses apologized, his voice breaking with emotion. "I didn't know the ball belonged to your boy. Take it to him."

Ajene snatched the ball from Moses's hand as he extended it above the unsightly wall.

Without another word, Ajene whirled and started

up the hill, angry that he'd have to add a stroke to his score to account for his errant shot into the rough. He didn't want to record the additional stroke. No one would be the wiser if he didn't.

Nevertheless, he was an honest man, he reminded himself, at least when it came to golf and things that really mattered.

* * * *

Ajene couldn't seem to keep his ball on the fairway for the remainder of the back nine at the Regal Kenyan. It was a challenging course for most golfers due to its rolling hills and irregular lines. But his problem wasn't just the lay of the land. He couldn't get his mind on the game.

What had he done? How dare he take something from a young boy that was clearly a source of glee in his otherwise bleak existence? What kind of man would lie to a child the way he did? And what about Moses? How was he doing now that he had no ball?

Ajene tried to rationalize his underhandedness

by telling himself that he hadn't asked Moses into his life. It wasn't his fault that the boy had found his golf ball. By simply walking away, he'd gotten Moses out of his world. If only he could get him off his mind.

Disgusted, Ajene stormed off the course near the sixteenth green. He headed for the clubhouse restaurant where he was unable to eat.

Again his thoughts turned to Moses, who was probably among the vast majority of Kiberan children who are rationed one donated meal, but only on school days. On weekends there's nothing to eat, and so they fast.

Ajene considered the integrity of a child who willingly gave up something he relished because it belonged to a youngster he didn't even know. He had fleeced that admirable boy.

Moses knew that Ajene was willing to buy the ball, but he didn't sell. When the issue became doing what was morally right, the poverty-stricken child gave back the ball free of charge.

Ajene didn't know any other children like that.

In fact, he didn't know any adults with that much character—including himself.

By sundown, the golfer's conscience was paining him in a way it never had. His mind visited places it hadn't in years. He thought of God and His Word, remembering that "a good name is more desirable than great riches; to be esteemed is better than silver or gold" (Prov. 22:1). He thought about children and virtuous things and how he, a successful businessman, had long ago forfeited the integrity a Kiberan child possessed.

Or maybe he hadn't lost it, Ajene considered sadly. Maybe he'd never had it in the first place.

His notions were runaway, as if someone else, or even a spirit, were controlling his mind. He even thought about the nutritious meals Americans provide to Kenya's starving, and how they regularly come so far at their own expense to give to people they don't even know. He wondered how anybody could care that much about strangers, and wished he cared that much about somebody.

"How do people acquire compassion?" he kept asking himself.

To Ajene, poor people had always been an inconvenience. They lived futile lives of trying to survive, with no hope for anything better. They could do nothing for him, so why help them?

But what about Moses? He gave away the only thing that brought him pleasure, making the sacrifice for a stranger who had everything. The child had derived more fulfillment from a cheap, unremarkable golf ball than Ajene felt amid all his possessions.

Ajene remembered something else about those American missionaries and humanitarian workers. They came to Africa in the name of Jesus Christ, the same Jesus they talked about during their meetings held in Nairobi's Uhuru Park. The men and women overflowed with joy when they talked about Jesus and always seemed as happy as Moses had seemed while the ball was in his possession. They called themselves Christians. They had a simple belief in their Savior that seemed to transcend life's complexities.

Ajene yearned to make sense of it. He closed his eyes to try to visualize all he'd seen in the Kiberan school yard. He vaguely recalled the tumbledown building that probably held classrooms. It all seemed so strange. His golf games had taken him past that structure many times, but he had never really noticed it. He realized now that seeing it so clearly made him uncomfortable, reminding him of all he had—and all that the countless children of Kibera did not.

Come Monday, Ajene decided, each would at least have their own golf ball. A rich man, poor in spirit, would see to that.

CHAPTER TWO

ONE CHILD THOUGHT IT WAS a hailstorm like those his teacher had described during a lesson about foreign weather. He wasn't sure, though. He'd never seen frozen rain.

Actually it was raining golf balls. Ajene was scooping them from a box and hurling them over the wall to the delight of Kiberan school children.

A few adults heard the laughter and emerged from their surrounding abodes. Some felt swept up by the excitement and wanted to gather balls for their own children. Others wondered what price these strange round things with dimples might bring on the streets of Nairobi.

Smiles beamed from teachers' faces, silently communicating to Ajene their gratitude for his generosity, although the women must have wondered how they'd settle the jubilant children in order to resume studies.

Watching from the other side of the wall, Ajene marveled at how generosity seemed to come naturally to the needy boys and girls. They were totally given to sharing, just as Moses had shared his golf ball with Ajene's "son," although he'd never met him.

A teacher announced that each child could have two balls, one for each pocket of his or her school uniform. She drew a circle in the dirt, and instructed children to set extra balls inside it.

Ajene was astonished to see perhaps a dozen balls placed inside the ring. Not one child was seen to be hording the extras. A single bulge protruded from each of their tandem pockets.

The donor had hoped that Moses might run to the fence to greet him. He missed the boy like he never thought he would.

He'd never previously thought so much about someone he'd known so briefly. He yearned to see him again.

Ajene assumed that Moses must be out there somewhere, camouflaged among other children with identical uniforms. But like the rest of the children, he must be too enthralled to focus on anything but the rolling playthings.

Ajene intensified his visual inventory of pupils, searching for the child whose unselfishness had tapped his conscience and prompted gifts for the entire student body.

But Moses was nowhere to be seen.

Ajene's scrutiny was continuing even as recess came to an end. Teachers were organizing children in a single file to march back to classrooms. Ajene didn't want Moses to reenter the schoolhouse without saying hello. He was determined to thank him for the display of kindness he'd shown the previous day. Ajene had held back two shiny golf balls especially for Moses. He wanted to present the gift personally.

He also wanted to confess the fact that he'd lied about having a son.

He waited until most of the children had returned to their classrooms, then summoned a teacher whose nametag read "Dalila."

As she turned to him, Ajene felt spellbound by her smile—a bright ear-to-ear beam that said thank you with greater eloquence than words could ever communicate. She confirmed what Ajene had suspected, that the balls he had given were the youngsters' only toys.

"Before you go back inside," Ajene requested, "I wonder if you'd mind asking Moses to come over here? I met him Friday. I don't know why he was on the playground by himself, but he was, and he returned my golf ball after it went over the fence."

"He was at the school on Friday evening going through the waste receptacles in back," the teacher told Ajene. "He was looking for food. He does this almost every weekend, but he doesn't find very much."

"I see," Ajene responded thoughtfully, sad to hear that such a benevolent boy was reduced to pilfering. "Would you mind sending him out so I can greet him?"

"He isn't here today," the teacher replied. "He's at home with Kamau and Nyah, his little brother and sister. They're too young for school. Moses will have to take care of them full-time now. I doubt that he'll return here, at least not this year."

"I don't understand" Ajene said. "Did his mother or father find work?"

"Moses has no father," Dalila replied. "His mother was very ill with AIDS. She died last night in her sleep."

Ajene stared blankly at Dalila, stricken dumb by her revelation. For some reason, he'd imagined that Moses had risen above Kibera's blight when he saw him happily playing with that golf ball. The boy gave no hint of any complaint in their exchange.

All the while, unknown to Ajene, Moses was laboring under the pressure to find food for his four-member family, including his dying mother.

Gripped by shame, Ajene turned his vacant gaze to the now empty school yard where Moses had frolicked two days ago. In his mind's eye he recalled the boy's filthy clothes beneath eyes that glistened.

Perhaps it had actually been tears he saw shining.

His reverie was broken by Dalila.

"Another teacher and I are going to Moses's house

with food after school," she said. "Would you like to come? You'll be safe in the light of day."

Ajene accepted without thinking. Otherwise he might have lacked the courage to ever enter Kibera.

* * * *

Dalila led the golfer into the schoolhouse, inviting him to visit its six classrooms. She wanted other teachers to introduce him to the children, whose squirming was unusually pronounced on this day, given the golf balls inside their pockets.

Met with bright smiles and applause in each room, Ajene realized the children's gratitude was as genuine as their innocence. Like Moses, none had ever seen a ball that was so small and totally firm. One little boy asked if the balls would grow bigger if buried underground.

In each classroom, at least one student asked to put his ear against Ajene's watch to hear it tick. And then another and another until teachers asked if Ajene minded the children forming a line to take turns listening. The task became an exercise in glee, and took up so much time that regular lessons weren't resumed on that special day.

Dalila had earlier sent two students with porridge to Moses's house. They returned in tears. A stranger had taken the food and had gulped it down in their presence, leaving them brokenhearted because Moses and his orphaned siblings would have nothing to eat.

She and the other teacher felt relieved when Ajene agreed to escort them with this afternoon's meal.

* * * *

Moses ran to Ajene in a way that went beyond excitement about their reunion. The boy wrapped his arms passionately around the golfer's neck with strength that belied his years. He didn't want to let go, and Ajene didn't force him.

Ajene recognized pain when he saw it. What could possibly hurt a boy more than the loss of his mother, his only known parent? What could frighten him more than inheriting the daunting task of rearing two younger siblings? Moses lived in one of the most desolate parts of the world, and the full weight of that desolation was crashing in on him. Clearly, he was buckling beneath the load.

The teachers pulled three bowls of porridge out of their paper bags, along with three spoons and as many containers of fresh water, part of an allotment bought regularly by the school from a Nairobi vendor, one of several haulers who helped alleviate the virtual absence of fresh water inside the slum.

Like all the other vendors, though, he charged five times as much as was charged to residents of Nairobi, and for a reason that everyone knew—simply because he could.

Moses, Kamau, and Nyah ate their food and drank moderately. There would be no other staples or water inside their hovel until, well, no one had thought about when. Moses had not pondered the future since last night when he heard his mother groan in a way she never had. Her labored breathing stopped, and she didn't answer when he called to her.

He had used a paper match to light a paraffin lamp that cast an eerie glow on her expressionless face, mouth and eyes gaped open. Moses crawled from his place on the dirt floor to her side. He touched her hand. It was cold. So was her face. He wrapped his arms around her while sobbing and pleading for her to respond. The more tightly he embraced her, the colder her body seemed.

Moses began to scream until a neighbor walked the few feet from her cardboard hut to his. The boy couldn't be silenced.

After a while two men appeared with blankets. Moses hoped they were doctors. They instead were among the detail that regularly removes Kiberans who die.

Moses wasn't told that these men, and others like them, work three daily shifts to rid the slum of its dead. He wouldn't have believed so many people are carried out day after day, having died of AIDS or diseases borne by the slum's filthy water.

The child didn't know where his mother was being taken. He knew only that she was gone.

Ajene promised Moses he'd find out the whereabouts of her body. He felt a quiet joy in making this vow to Moses that he was determined to keep, although he wondered how.

> Commit to the LORD whatever you do, and
> your plans will succeed.
> —PROVERBS 16:3

Honoring his word would help Ajene purge his own conscience of the guilt he felt in having previously deceived Moses about the golf ball. He was determined to redeem himself.

Ajene felt surprised to find himself becoming thoughtful and melancholy. His mind wandered back through the years to the teachings of an American missionary. The golfer had never subscribed to the minister's opinions about salvation. Nonetheless, he began to recall the preacher's telling of the biblical story about the good Samaritan:

> On one occasion an expert in the law stood
> up to test Jesus. "Teacher," he asked, "what
> must I do to inherit eternal life?"
>
> "What is written in the Law?" he replied.
> "How do you read it?"

> He answered: "'Love the Lord your God with
> all you heart and with all your soul and with
> all your strength and with all your mind',
> and, 'Love your neighbor as yourself.'"
>
> "You have answered correctly," Jesus replied.
> "Do this and you will live."
> —LUKE 10:25–28

Ajene was himself a lawyer. He'd never realized, until right then, that *eternal* carried two meanings. One was obviously life without end. But that was not the *eternal* Jesus was referring to. He was speaking in terms of the alternate definition, which describes the quality of one's life experience. Jesus was basically saying that whenever a person finds someone in need, he should reach out to them—just as the Samaritan had done. The reaching out is an act of love that knows no boundaries. And the bliss one feels in doing this way creates warm, good feelings that are like the joy of eternal life.

Ajene's mind began to run away with him. He thought about how his career achievements had brought wealth and placed him among Nairobi's elite. He wondered if his social standing would be as distinguished in faraway America. He wondered if wealthy Americans were as unhappy as he.

He'd read a story once about an American who said he'd climbed the ladder of success only to realize that he'd propped his ladder against the wrong building. The golfer thought about all of the United States' show business personalities whose extreme behavior was reported in the African press. The celebrities were as unfulfilled by their wealth as he was with his, he surmised.

"Why," he thought, "are they forever turning to alcohol and drugs? Would I do the same if I lived in America where that kind of behavior is acceptable among the rich?"

Ajene had always believed in God, but he'd never approached Him. His attitude had been that God should help the poor people who needed help, not him, a wealthy man who needed nothing.

But he *did* need something after all—suddenly he knew.

He needed peace like that he saw in Moses, a child who had nothing. Ajene compared Moses's authen-

44

ticity to his own outward show of happiness, which was mostly pretense despite his having "everything," at least as the world defined it. Why would a man who has everything obsess over a lost golf ball? And why would such a man lie to an impoverished and disadvantaged child in order to get it back?

"What have I become?" Ajene said to no one. He thought about all of the advantages wealth afforded him, while the grip of poverty pulled people like Moses down. His attitude had always been, "I've got mine; too bad for you."

Ajene knew his thinking was about to change. He felt wellsprings of joy and compassion bubbling up into places where he'd felt nothing for years. For the first time within memory he found himself laughing spontaneously. He sensed he was on the brink of something great, and he just had to chuckle at the irony. Losing the golf ball had been such a small matter in the scheme of things. But it had provided the gateway to this life-changing experience. His soul was beginning to fill, as if his was the joy of a modern-day Good Samaritan.

✶ ✶ ✶ ✶

The teachers told Moses they'd return to his hut with more food around the same time tomorrow. Dalila promised more vegetables along with the porridge. She examined what remained of the water, and reminded Moses that's all there would be until she came back.

It was getting late. Dalila and the other teacher had their own families to attend. As the women departed the lean-to, each looked at Ajene with fearful eyes that posed a silent question: Could he stay and care for these crestfallen children?

Ajene astonished himself when he said he'd volunteer.

✶ ✶ ✶ ✶

The women had been gone for only a few minutes when Ajene began feeling the ominous pressure of his responsibility. What had he done? Why had he allowed himself to succumb to the children's pleading stares? Did they think that he was going to step in and take over their parenting? Why?

Their circumstances were dire, Ajene conceded. But weren't everyone's in Kibera? These were not the first children to lose their mother to AIDS, or the first to be left alone. What do the others do? Can't these orphans do the same?

Ajene's panicky thoughts were runaway as he and the three children sat on an earthen floor, deep in the bowels of Kibera. He had simply wanted to be nice to Moses, not inherit his misery. He didn't want to walk out on the distressed children, but he didn't want to stay. How could he rationalize a heartless departure? What could he say to console the three tiny faces fixed on his?

"These children are going to have it rough without their mother and they might as well start getting use to it" was the best he could come up with.

"Besides," he continued rationalizing, "They've already been roughing it to a certain extent. How much nurturing could their sick mother have provided? She'd been immobilized by AIDS for some time. And no doubt she was inattentive while suffering her agonizing death. Moses is probably accustomed to generating income for the household."

Ajene knew his thoughts were jaded. Still, he needed to know just how Moses had been subsidizing the family. Anything the child told him might ease his conscious. So he told Moses, point blank, to stop crying and to talk to him about money.

He learned that Moses went to a Kiberan dump on weekends where he worked alongside other children and old women to recover plastic bags to recycle. If he worked from sunrise to sundown, he could unearth a pound of plastic worth sixty-seven shillings. He could repeat the scenario the next day, and derive another sixty-seven.

With regard to food, Moses had learned how to "push the week," with *sukuma wiki*, a dish made from collard greens or kale. It could be purchased for three shillings per bunch, which allowed the child to feed the family for seven days.

And as for water—before school each Monday through Friday, Moses walked to the place where the man from Nairobi sold clean water. The water, like the other household bills, had been paid for by his mother with money she earned by way of her secret treatment, Moses told Ajene.

"What do you mean by 'secret treatment'?" Ajene asked.

"Men came after dark and visited Mother," Moses explained. "My brother, sister, and I were asleep when they came, and they always left before we got up. Mother said we were never to tell about their visits—they were a secret. The men gave her shillings to get her treatment."

Ajene said nothing. He'd heard that Kiberan women, even those with AIDS, prostitute themselves with drunken and depraved men. He'd been told that prostitutes often rendered their services with children sleeping in the same room, as the mud shanties have no divided spaces.

Moses said two men had come last night for his mother's treatment. He didn't think they'd left shillings, though, as he'd heard one say she wasn't breathing. The men accidentally awakened Moses, but were gone by the time he lit his paraffin lamp. He was going to ask his mother if she was done with the treatment, but she didn't answer. That's when he discovered she was lifeless.

Ajene was hearing the most horrific story he'd ever heard.

An unsuspecting child had lost his mother during the very act of prostitution by which she kept her family alive!

Nightfall comes abruptly near the equator. Ajene hadn't noticed its encroachment as the darkness outside blended with the darkness inside the orphans' nine-by-nine windowless habitat. He realized how much he'd been engrossed in the situation when he stepped from the shelter and was swallowed by the black Kiberan night.

Terror seized him like a vice.

He had unwittingly become a prisoner of darkness that prohibited safe travel along the paths that would take him out of Kibera. If he ventured out to walk them, no doubt he would be robbed. Worse yet, he might be injured or killed. Kibera was a place of two cultures—one of the daytime, the other of the night. The night people preyed violently on the daytime's working class, who hunkered in their shelters until sunrise. Ajene knew he wasn't going anywhere until dawn brought hundreds of thousands of Kiberans out of their houses, when the safety of numbers would once again prevail.

Ajene looked rich—and he *was* rich—with coordinated clothes that would stand out among destitute and desperate men now shuffling in shadows outside Moses's abode. Ajene had more shillings in his wallet than most Kiberans see in years.

Nothing stood to protect him from Kibera's criminal element now except three children and a cardboard door. He was stuck and couldn't leave if he expected to be safe, at least not until the morning light.

He asked Moses to light the candle. The glow of light, however faint, would help him believe he had a hint of protection against those on the other side of the flimsy wall.

Ajene was unaware of one of the most heinous criminal practices in Kibera, the robbing of a home when its inhabitants were thought to be viewing their dead or preparing their funeral. He'd read that most armed robberies happen over the weekend after the last Friday of the month, when workers have cashed their paychecks. This month's final Friday was three days ago. The time for such a robbery was ripe, and Ajene was suddenly fearful to the bone.

It was then that he really began to notice the terri-fying sounds of Kibera after dark, agonizing noises that rose from inside the tumbledown shanties and drifted through the stagnant air around them. It was a sick concert of guttural expressions from drug and alcohol crazed men and their victims.

Ajene was astonished at Moses's oblivion to all of it. He'd heard the drone of this madness every night of his short life. His only concern seemed to be that Ajene take him, his brother and his sister to see their deceased mother tomorrow, as prom-ised. Ajene repeated his vow to do so. Then he was amazed to see Moses lie down on the hard dirt floor beside his siblings and drift immediately off to sleep.

Utterly alone, Ajene felt the full extent of his

vulnerability inside a makeshift residence within the depths of what was perhaps Kenya's most dangerous place.

"How did I let this happen to me?" he asked himself.

There was no answer except the sickening sounds of Kibera at night.

Ajene lay down beside his unwittingly adopted family, whose soft breathing was a peaceful contrast to the haunting violence leaking in from outside. Ajene heard men cursing loudly in an attempt to silence the pleading from women they were raping. Pressing his hands over his ears, he couldn't keep out the sounds of suffering.

Feeling desperate, Ajene ripped open his shirt. He tied it around his head like a turban, hoping the cloth against his ears might muffle the sounds. It didn't.

Morbid curiosity urged him to peek outside, but he was afraid. He hoped that none of the human predators had seen him enter the home, that he and the children would be safe. He'd taken care to not draw attention to himself when coming here. Perhaps he wouldn't be bothered when leaving.

Who was he kidding? Ajene knew he was a conspicuous stranger in a strange land. His coming had undoubtedly caused a buzz of excited discussion. A well-dressed man wearing a watch and jewelry had entered the ramshackled shanty of a dead prostitute whose body had earlier been removed. Of course Kiberans were watching the place. Ajene felt as if all of Kibera knew of his vulnerability.

He began feeling sick from stress. His attempts at self-consolation were not working. If he had no control over his own mind, how could he expect to defend himself and three sleeping children? It was another question for which he had no answer.

For the first time in years, Ajene began to pray, begging God to get him out alive. He recalled with shame his earlier thoughts of abandoning the youngsters. He asked God to forgive him. He'd heard it said that God uses imperfect men. He certainly hoped so. Given the years he'd wasted in self-absorption, he was nothing if not imperfect.

"If God uses men like me, surely He protects them too," Ajene thought, desperate for hope.

Instinctively, he tried to bargain with God. "Lord, if you'll get me out of here, I'll take these children with me." His promise, though arrogant he realized, did have a sincere tone of repentance. Ajene no longer thought of saving himself by fleeing the helpless little ones—not tonight, not ever.

Then just outside the shelter he heard voices, low voices of maybe two or three men.

"He's still in there," whispered one.

"I'll cut him. You take his money," another said. "Do it right, so he can't ever say it was us."

Ajene recalled having seen a newspaper story about thieves who, while high on *bhang* (marijuana) and *Chang'aa* (alcohol), were cutting people to get them to hand over their money. They cut them fatally if they didn't get enough.

Ajene knew that his life was in danger. He needed something to distract the assailants, something that would take their focus off him.

A solution came to him so quickly, he was

sure it had come from God. Everyone knew that Kiberans feared one thing above all else—a fire. A stray flame could instantly engulf any shanty in Kibera like a tinderbox, turning the entire slum into a raging inferno.

Ajene determined to use fire as a deterrent. "But how?" he asked himself. He had always thought best while standing. He rose to his feet as straight as the low roof would allow, frantically searching his pockets for...something. He wasn't sure what. He needed anything he could use to threaten or start a blaze.

He fished out a tiny aerosol can of breath freshener no larger than a roll of American Life Savers candy. Alcohol was the container's key ingredient. *Alcohol is extremely flammable,* he reminded himself.

Emboldened by his find, Ajene eased back to the floor, bracing for anyone who might bolt through the door. The malevolent whispers were drawing ever closer.

Ajene nudged Moses gently with his foot. The sleeping boy responded with only a slight stir and a snore. Ajene then gave him a more determined shove.

Moses bolted upright, alarmed and disoriented.

"Silence!" Ajene whispered insistently, leaning directly into the child's ear. "Silence!"

He felt sure Moses would soon notice the hostile talk just outside the door. It didn't take him long. As Moses opened his mouth to scream, Ajene stifled him with the palm of his hand.

"They've come to harm us," Ajene whispered, his hand still across Moses's mouth. "We must all leave here and never return."

Moses put his hand on Ajene's and gently tugged, indicating that he could remove his palm.

"I know ways out of Kibera you don't know," Moses whispered. "Darkness doesn't stop me."

Ajene stared at the boy in amazement, but not for long.

The invaders were going to come through the door any second. At least one had a knife, and intended to use it.

"Slide your brother and sister to me," Ajene hurriedly instructed. "I'll carry them, following you."

Moses nodded his understanding.

With that, Ajene raised the paraffin lamp, placed the aerosol can behind its flame and pressed the button. It was like a pocket-size flamethrower. The combustible mist burst into a jet of flames, spreading itself against the arid walls. Immediately the cardboard shack was transformed into a fireball. Moses bolted through the thin wall of flames with Ajene close behind, toting a child under each arm. Outside, the night was a mass of hysteria and confusion. The occupants of nearby shanties frantically tore down their wood and paper walls, carrying the materials out of harm's way in a chaotic process they underwent any time a neighboring shanty caught fire. No one noticed the man and three children who were running and kept running—away from the fire, away from Kibera.

CHAPTER THREE

AJENE CONTACTED AN UNDERTAKER WHO routinely buried Kibera's indigent. Ajene, Dalila, Moses, and his two siblings were the only people at the graveside when the mother was lowered into the parched earth.

After the internment, Moses returned to Ajene's home, where he, his brother, and sister had stayed for three days since the fire had saved them from the intruders. Since arriving at Ajene's, all of the children had slept in one bed. For the first time in their lives, they'd danced inside an indoor shower and used soap from a store to wash their bodies. The tile floor was covered with smudges and dark puddles. Ajene asked each child to bathe again until dirt no longer covered the drain.

It was a happy time. Ajene lovingly teased the

naïve children, telling them that a shower was indoor rainfall that could be made at any time. None had known that "rain" could fall under a roof. The children soon came to enjoy bathing so much that they did so without being told.

More than anything, Moses wanted to meet Ajene's son, the boy to whom he'd surrendered his golf ball. Maybe, he thought, they could play with it together before Moses returned to Kibera.

"Where is your boy?" Moses asked Ajene.

Feeling a mountain of pain and embarrassment, the golfer finally replied, "I hope I'm looking at him."

Moses eyed him quizzically. "I don't understand."

"Moses, I lied," Ajene confessed with sadness. "I wanted you to return my golf ball the day we first met. When I saw your concern for others, I thought you'd give it back if I said my son wanted the ball. But I have no son. I tricked you just to get what I wanted for myself."

Moses stared at Ajene, who read the confusion in the boy's eyes. He knew the child couldn't comprehend how anyone could want anything badly enough to deceive. He marveled at the character Moses' late mother had instilled in her children. He felt remorse that someone so noble had been desperate enough to sell her suffering body in order to provide for her children.

In the space of thirty-six hours, Moses had been given a prize that was taken away, his mother had died in her sleep, and strange men had come for her body. And the ordeal had ended with the burning of the only home he had ever known. Then the displaced boy had surrendered his siblings to a grown man whom he had led on a terrified sprint over treacherous paths to escape Kibera.

Somehow the child seemed remarkably composed. In fact, he seemed at home under Ajene's loving care. During that fiery night, Ajene had seen in Moses the fear he felt himself. But he never heard the lad complain, and he never saw him put himself before his brother or sister.

"Moses, I talked you into surrendering that ball because I only cared about my silly game," Ajene told him. "I have many possessions, and I am accustomed to getting what I want. I didn't want to let you interrupt my game by keeping the ball."

It was clear to Ajene that the child simply couldn't relate—either to being accustomed to getting what he wanted or to the selfishness such privilege had inspired in Ajene.

"Moses, you have suffered all of your life. You haven't been aware of it because suffering has been the normal for everyone around you. Despite your suffering, though, you've been a happy person. I watched you laugh on that day at the schoolyard, and I wished I could be as happy as you."

"I'll help you be happy," the boy said as he remembered a Bible verse. It was the longest his mother had ever taught him.

> I am not saying this because I am in need, for I have learned to be content whatever the circumstances. I know what it is to be in need, and I know what it is to have plenty. I have learned the secret of being content in any and every situation, whether well fed or hungry, whether living in plenty or in want.

I can do everything through him who gives
me strength.
                              —PHILIPPIANS 4:11–13

"You already have helped me to be happy," Ajene said. "You've brought me happiness just as surely as you saved my life when you led us out of Kibera."

"God didn't give me a son," Ajene added, "but if He did, I wish it would have been you."

"Me too," Moses said.

The boy looked upward into eyes filled with tears. Ajene had once recognized Moses' pain. Now, Moses saw in Ajene the deep pain of his loneliness.

"Will you and your brother and sister live with me and be my family?" Ajene asked. "You'll go to a public school and live in this house," Ajene continued. "We'll have to go through many meetings with other adults before I can adopt you—which means, to make you my own children."

"You would do that for us?" Moses asked.

"I will," the would-be father replied.

"But why?" Moses responded.

"When I lost my golf ball, I found my life," replied Ajene.

Ajene wondered if Moses would ever speak.

"Would you teach me to play golf like you?" the boy asked.

"Of course," said the golfer. "And the ball you found will be your first."

With that, Ajene produced the ball he had swindled from Moses on their first encounter. He had already inscribed "Moses" on its bumpy surface.

The child grinned with unreserved joy in the way that only children do. Ajene had never seen such a look on the boy whose childhood had previously been surrendered so he could become the "man of the house." Now the little man could resume his childhood enjoying a home complete with a grownup dad.

Ajene felt the warm smarting of tears gathering in his eyes as he stared long and lovingly at Moses and his siblings. "I have found my life," he whispered to himself. "My life is made complete and purposeful by the taking care of others—the taking care of these children."

And so began a new quest for the golfer, Ajene, and for Moses and his siblings. Theirs was now a life that for the first time included regular meals, ample clothes, plentiful love, and the truly amazing magic of indoor rain.

EPILOGUE

Everyone who competes in the games goes into strict training. They do it to get a crown that will not last; but we do it to get a crown that will last forever.
—1 CORINTHIANS 9:25

THE BOOK YOU'VE JUST READ IS FICTION THAT ends happily, but it portrays real situations that don't.

The slum in which Moses and his siblings lived—Kibera—is an informal settlement whose name means "forest" or "jungle." It originated in 1920 as a Nubian soldiers' outpost and is situated just outside the prominent capital city of Nairobi, adjacent to a posh Nairobi golf club. With the serene Ngong Hills and a riot of colorful trees and flowers serving as a backdrop, the 7,021-yard, par seventy-two course is a popular playground for Kenya's richest citizens. It is, perhaps, the most beautiful golf course in the entire country. No wonder the golfers simply avert their eyes to avoid seeing Kibera's shanties made of mud, cardboard, and corrugated sheet metal. The average American duck blind is sturdier than these makeshift structures and offers greater protection from the elements. The flimsy cardboard falls in on itself. The rusty, crumbling sheet metal resembles the brown, fishy scales of rotting carp tied together with wire or string.

Almost a million people subsist on Kibera's approximate 550 acres, making it a place of bewildering complexity, confusion, and struggle—a true-to-life "human jungle" befitting the settlement's name. The density averages about two thousand people per acre. They can grow nothing on the barren land. It yields only the stench of rot and excrement.

Running water and sanitation are virtually nonexistent. The settlement offers a total of about six hundred toilets—which means that most residents are forced to urinate on the ground and to use plastic bags when voiding their bowels. When done, they hurl the filthy sacks into the air. The refuse comes down with a splat wherever trajectory takes it. It's hard to live in Kibera and not, at some point, be hit by a "flying toilet."

Every day a host of Kiberans, mostly women and young girls, form lines at sunrise to buy water at roadside standpipes. Private sellers pump limited supplies, for which they charge three to thirty cents for a twenty-liter jerry can. Because of the high price they are charged, most Kiberans simply can't afford to buy water. Thus, they are left with two options: 1) drink the water standing in a filthy ditch that weaves throughout the compound—water so rank that decaying animals and fecal matter can be seen floating in it; or 2) simply go without. Death from dehydration is the number-one killer of Kiberans.

In addition to dehydration, the AIDS pandemic looms over daily life in Africa. More than 12 million African children are orphans because of AIDS. Their numbers increase daily. The majority are as desperate as Moses. For them, there is no "Ajene."

But there is hope. You can help get food, medicine, and a chance for an education to children who otherwise might not have a life.

Your tax-deductible donations may be sent to:

Feed The Children
P. O. Box 78
Oklahoma City, OK 73101

Check our Web site at www.feedthechildren.org to see which of our many humanitarian efforts you'd like to address, whether in Africa, America, or other parts of the world. Our e-mail address is ftc@feedthechildren.org.

You may also reach our main office by calling (800) 627-4556. Our office hours are Monday through Friday, 8:00 a.m. to 5:00 p.m. (CST).

All royalties from this book go to support *Feed The Children's AIDS Orphans Projects.*

The majority of Feed The Children's donors will never find their way into the horrific world of child suffering, but your contributions ensure that millions of children will find their way out.

—Larry Jones

Founder and President, Feed The Children